Published by Images Press

Publisher's Cataloging-in-Publication
   (Provided by Quality Books, Inc.)

   Trimble, Marcia.
      Liberty Cafe is open / written by Marcia Trimble ; illustrated by Jennifer Hayden. — 1st ed.
      p. cm.
      SUMMARY: A surprise birthday party on Miss Henny Penny's houseboat is the highlight of Alice Ann's vacation with Uncle Spurge.
      Audience: Ages 4-8.
      LCCN 2005909254
      ISBN-13: 978-1-891577-90-1 (hc)
      ISBN-10: 1-891577-90-5 (hc)
      ISBN-13: 978-1-891577-91-8 (pbk.)
      ISBN-10: 1-891577-91-3 (pbk.)

      1. Surprise birthday parties—Juvenile fiction.
   [1. Birthdays—Fiction. 2. Parties—Fiction.]   I. Hayden, Jennifer. II. Title.

   PZ7.T7352Li 2006   [E]
                  QBI05-200198

   10 9 8 7 6 5 4 3 2 1

Repeat text set in Pie Contest. Cartoon text set in Mister Sirloin.
Book design by Sprague Design.
Manufactured in China by South China Printing Co. Ltd.
Printed on chlorine-free paper.

To my sister, Alice.
—M.T.

For Mom, who never made me set the table
when I was drawing.
—Jennifer Hayden

ding dong "Liberty Cafe is open!"
Miss Henny Penny's Liberty Bell
rings in the morning... ding dong

S-T-R-E-T-C-H...Y-A-W-N

and everyone is waiting for Alice Ann.

The red, white, and blue flag flutters
over 51 Liberty Dock!

☆The bell rings... ding dong

and everyone is waiting for Alice Ann.

WHAT SHOULD I WEAR?
S-T-R-E-T-C-H...P-U-L-L

Annabelle, the cat, meows
through the early mist!

☆The flag flutters... ☆The bell rings... ding dong

and everyone is waiting for Alice Ann.

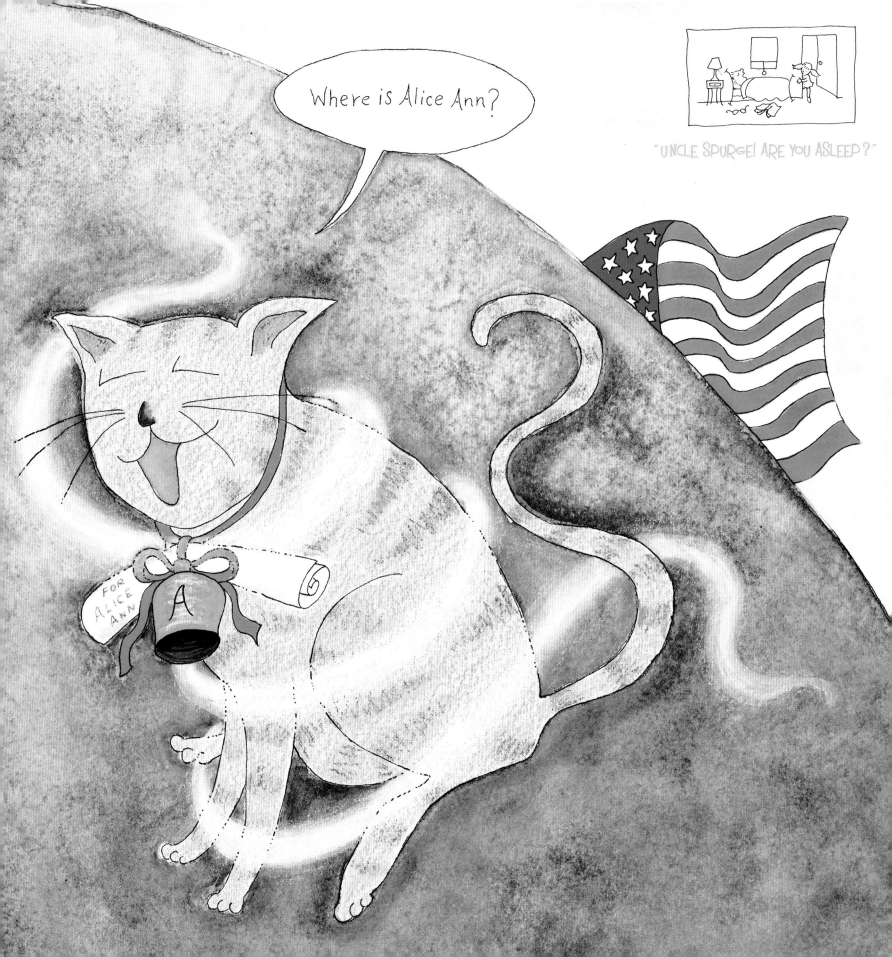

The daisies in the planter box
smile at the peeking sun!
☆The cat meows... ☆The flag flutters...
☆The bell rings... ding dong
and everyone is waiting for Alice Ann.

Abner, the dog, barks at the day!
☆The daisies smile... ☆The cat meows...
☆The flag flutters... ☆The bell rings... ding dong
and everyone is waiting for Alice Ann,

Miss Henny Penny stirs
the batter of Penny Pancakes!
✩The dog barks... ✩The daisies smile...
✩The cat meows... ✩The flag flutters...
✩The bell rings... ding dong
and everyone is waiting for Alice Ann.

The sausage sizzles in the griddle!

☆ Miss Henny Penny stirs...

☆ The dog barks...

☆ The daisies smile...

☆ The cat meows... ☆ The flag flutters...

☆ The bell rings... ding dong

and everyone is waiting for Alice Ann.

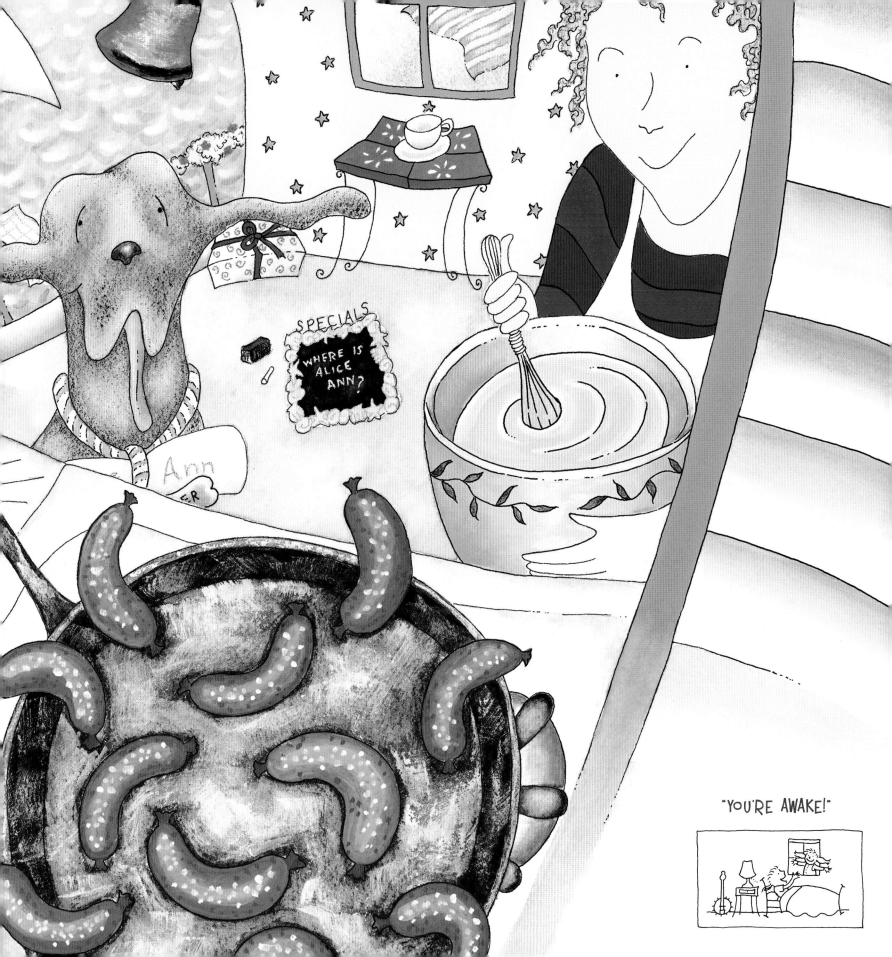

"YOU'RE AWAKE!"

The houseboaters cheer, "Breakfast's in the air!"
☆The sausage sizzles... ☆Miss Henny Penny stirs...
☆The dog barks... ☆The daisies smile...
☆The cat meows... ☆The flag flutters...
☆The bell rings... ding dong
and everyone is waiting for Alice Ann.

Gilly, the gull, calls through the curling smoke!

☆The houseboaters cheer... ☆The sausage sizzles...

☆Miss Henny Penny stirs... ☆The dog barks...

☆The daisies smile... ☆The cat meows...

☆The flag flutters... ☆The bell rings... ding dong

and everyone is waiting for Alice Ann.

It's Alice Ann!

Voilà! Alice Ann wins the race to Liberty Cafe.

★ The gull calls...   ★ The houseboaters cheer...

★ The sausage sizzles...

★ Miss Henny Penny stirs...   ★ The dog barks...

★ The daisies smile...   ★ The cat meows...

★ The flag flutters...

★ The bell rings...ding dong

and no one is waiting for Alice Ann!

Good morning, Miss Henny Penny!"
call Uncle Spurge and Alice Ann.

Wishes can come true!

THANK YOU!

YOU'RE INVITED

TO A PARTY

Party cards!

✧ Download.
✧ Print out from computer.
✧ Give to your friends for your next party.

Have fun!

Images-press.com
Book page
Liberty Cafe Is Open
Party cards link

Trimble Tots Collection

images press
for the young at heart

www.images-press.com